My Little Pony
Friendship is Magic
Vol. 6

WRITTEN BY **Heather Nuhfer**

ART BY **Amy Mebberson**

COLORS BY **Heather Breckel**

LETTERS BY **Neil Uyetake**

EDITED BY **Bobby Curnow**

ABDO Spotlight

IDW

ABDOPUBLISHING.COM

Reinforced library bound edition published in 2016 by Spotlight, a division of ABDO, PO Box 398166, Minneapolis, Minnesota 55439. Spotlight produces high-quality reinforced library bound editions for schools and libraries. Published by agreement with IDW.

Printed in the United States of America, North Mankato, Minnesota.
042015
092015

THIS BOOK CONTAINS RECYCLED MATERIALS

Licensed By:

LIBRARY OF CONGRESS CATALOGING-IN-PUBLICATION DATA

Cook, Katie, 1981-
My little pony : friendship is magic / writer, Katie Cook ; artist, Andy Price ; colors, Heather Breckel ; letters, Robbie Robbins and Neil Uyetake. -- Reinforced library bound edition.
8 volumes ; cm
Volumes 1-4 written by Katie Cook, illustrated by Andy Price -- Volumes 5-8 written by Heather Nuhfer, illustrated by Amy Mebberson.
ISBN 978-1-61479-376-2 (v. 1) -- ISBN 978-1-61479-377-9 (v. 2) -- ISBN 978-1-61479-378-6 (v. 3) -- ISBN 978-1-61479-379-3 (v. 4) -- ISBN 978-1-61479-380-9 (v. 5) -- ISBN 978-1-61479-381-6 (v. 6) -- ISBN 978-1-61479-382-3 (v. 7) -- ISBN 978-1-61479-383-0 (v. 8)
1. Graphic novels. I. Price, Andy, illustrator. II. Nuhfer, Heather, author. III. Mebberson, Amy ; illustrator. IV. My little pony, friendship is magic (Television program) V. Title. VI. Title: Friendship is magic.
PZ7.7.C666My 2016
741.5'973--dc23

2015001976

Spotlight

A Division of ABDO
abdopublishing.com

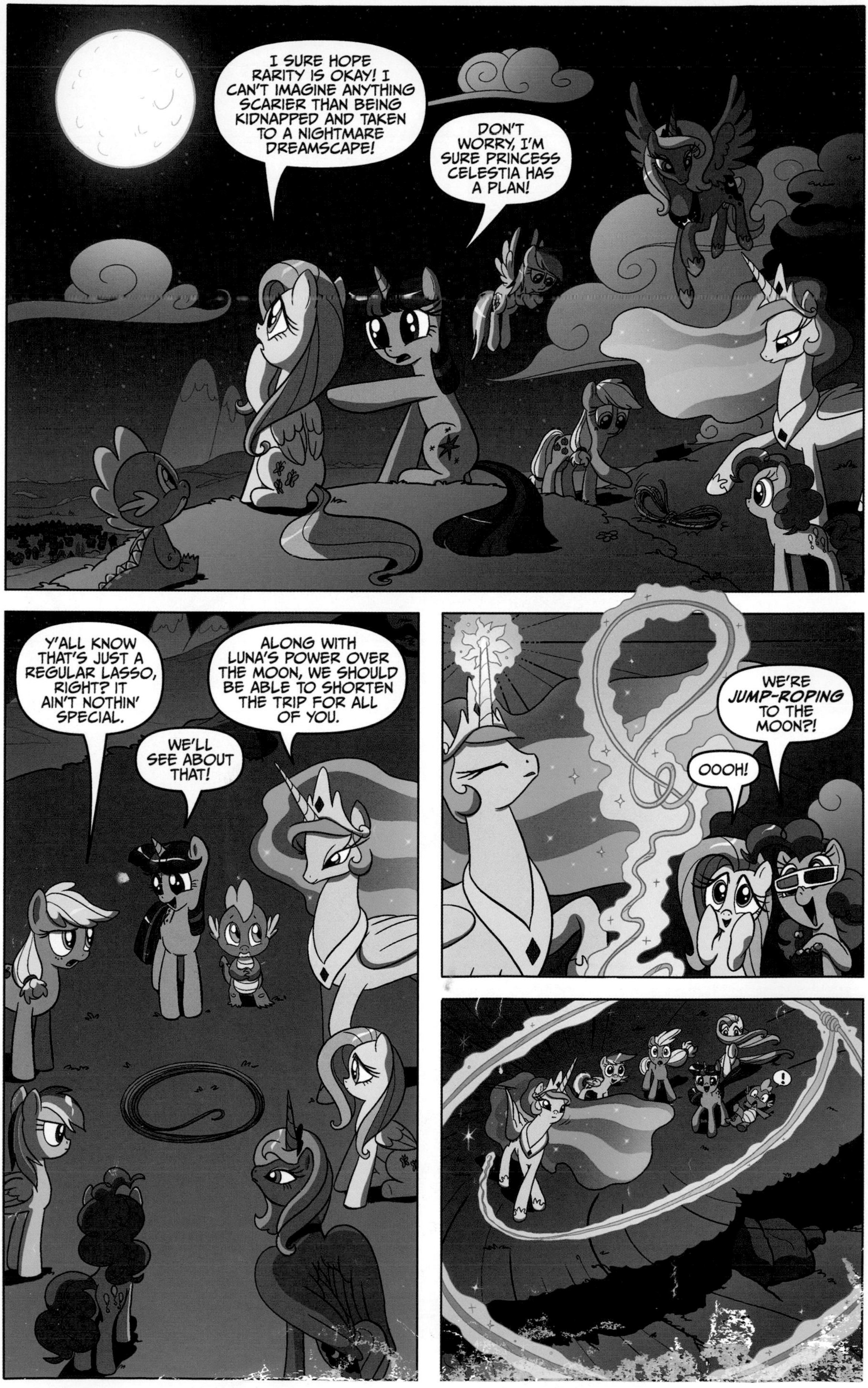
I SURE HOPE RARITY IS OKAY! I CAN'T IMAGINE ANYTHING SCARIER THAN BEING KIDNAPPED AND TAKEN TO A NIGHTMARE DREAMSCAPE!
DON'T WORRY, I'M SURE PRINCESS CELESTIA HAS A PLAN!
Y'ALL KNOW THAT'S JUST A REGULAR LASSO, RIGHT? IT AIN'T NOTHIN' SPECIAL.
WE'LL SEE ABOUT THAT!
ALONG WITH LUNA'S POWER OVER THE MOON, WE SHOULD BE ABLE TO SHORTEN THE TRIP FOR ALL OF YOU.
WE'RE *JUMP-ROPING* TO THE MOON?!
OOOH!
!

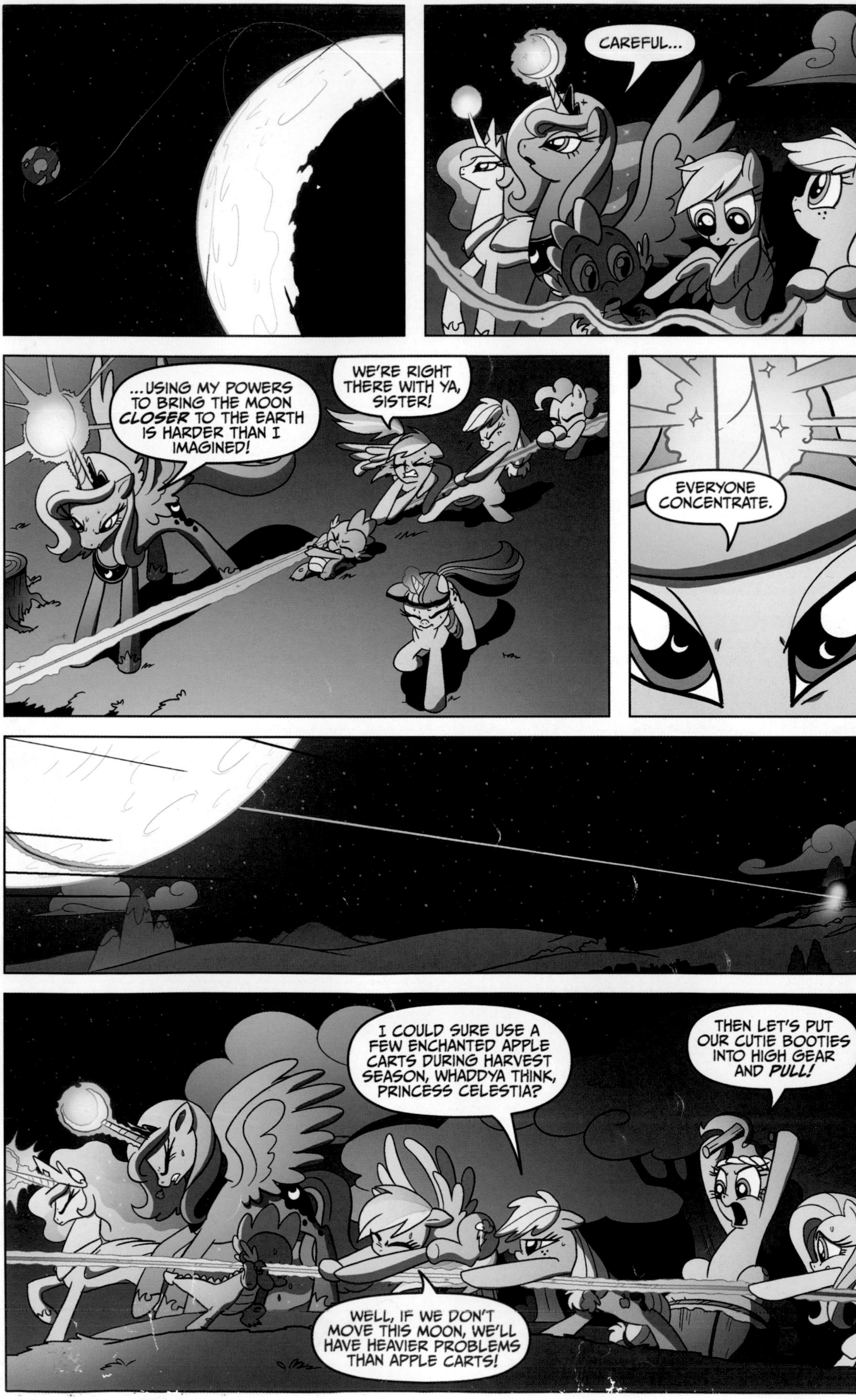
CAREFUL...
...USING MY POWERS TO BRING THE MOON CLOSER TO THE EARTH IS HARDER THAN I IMAGINED!
WE'RE RIGHT THERE WITH YA, SISTER!
EVERYONE CONCENTRATE.
I COULD SURE USE A FEW ENCHANTED APPLE CARTS DURING HARVEST SEASON, WHADDYA THINK, PRINCESS CELESTIA?
THEN LET'S PUT OUR CUTIE BOOTIES INTO HIGH GEAR AND PULL!
WELL, IF WE DON'T MOVE THIS MOON, WE'LL HAVE HEAVIER PROBLEMS THAN APPLE CARTS!

BONK!

THAT'S IT! WELL DONE, MY PONIES. I WILL BEGIN TO PREPARE PONYVILLE. GOOD LUCK!

THE WINGLESS PONIES WILL HAVE TO USE SURE FOOTING...

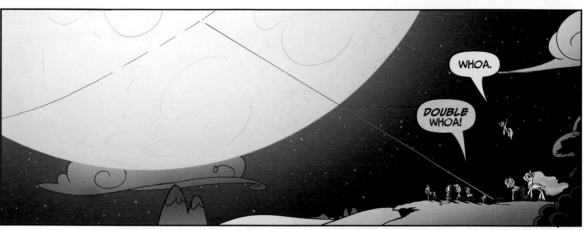

WHOA.

DOUBLE WHOA!

THIS IS YOUR LAST CHANCE TO CHANGE YOUR MINDS. REMEMBER, THE DARK FORCES THAT TOOK RARITY WILL USE ALL OF THEIR POWER TO SCARE YOU. THEY WILL UNRAVEL YOU WITH YOUR GREATEST FEARS.

HOPEFULLY IT'S NOT TOO LATE...

WHEN WE'RE TOGETHER, THE ELEMENTS OF HARMONY CAN OVERCOME ANYTHING.

AS LONG AS WE GET RARITY BACK, IT'LL ALL TURN OUT JUST DANDY.

LET'S DO THIS!

KLOP-SPROIIING

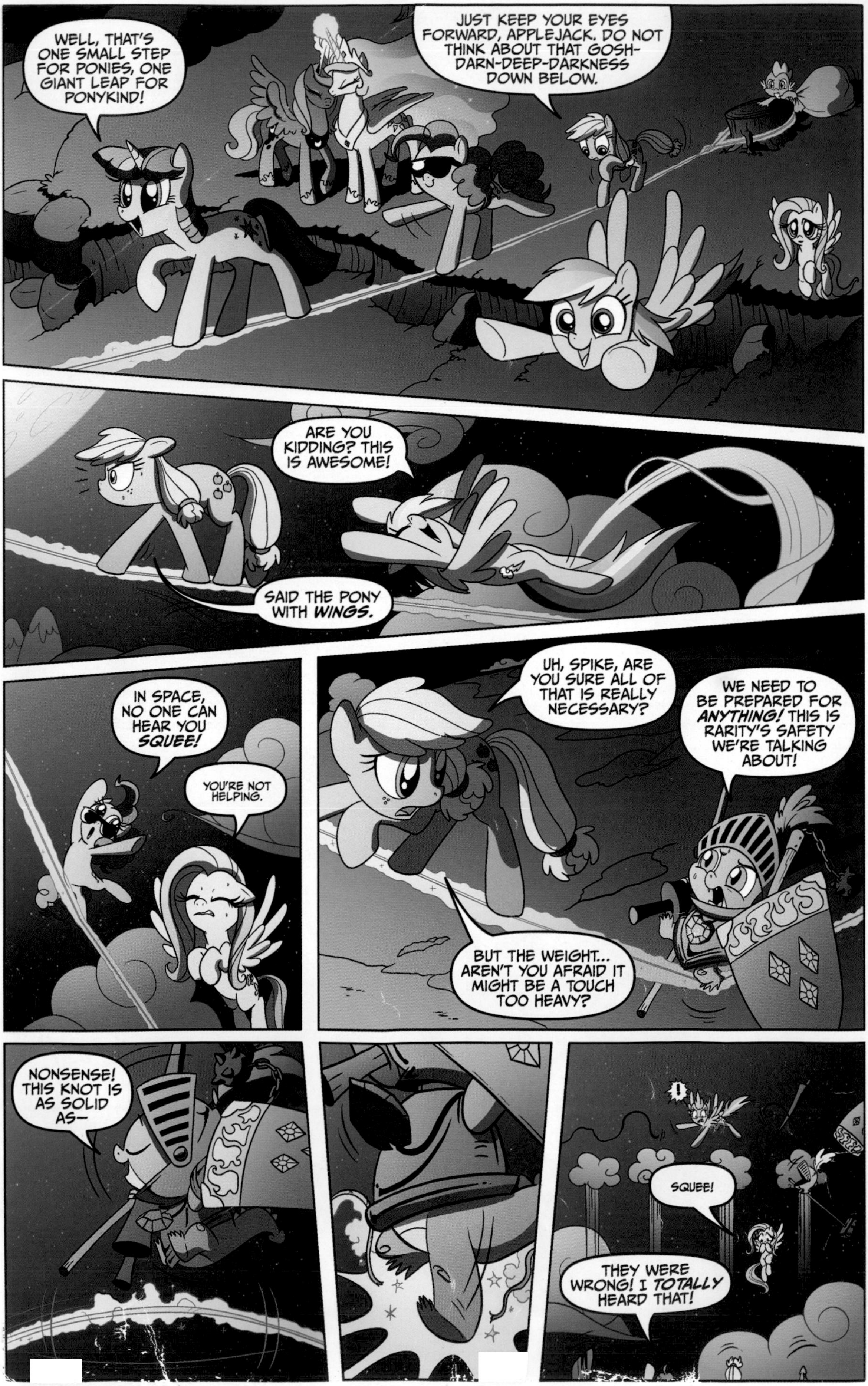
WELL, THAT'S ONE SMALL STEP FOR PONIES, ONE GIANT LEAP FOR PONYKIND!
JUST KEEP YOUR EYES FORWARD, APPLEJACK. DO NOT THINK ABOUT THAT GOSH-DARN-DEEP-DARKNESS DOWN BELOW.
ARE YOU KIDDING? THIS IS AWESOME!
SAID THE PONY WITH *WINGS.*
IN SPACE, NO ONE CAN HEAR YOU *SQUEE!*
YOU'RE NOT HELPING.
UH, SPIKE, ARE YOU SURE ALL OF THAT IS REALLY NECESSARY?
WE NEED TO BE PREPARED FOR *ANYTHING!* THIS IS RARITY'S SAFETY WE'RE TALKING ABOUT!
BUT THE WEIGHT... AREN'T YOU AFRAID IT MIGHT BE A TOUCH TOO HEAVY?
NONSENSE! THIS KNOT IS AS SOLID AS—
!
SQUEE!
THEY WERE WRONG! I *TOTALLY* HEARD THAT!

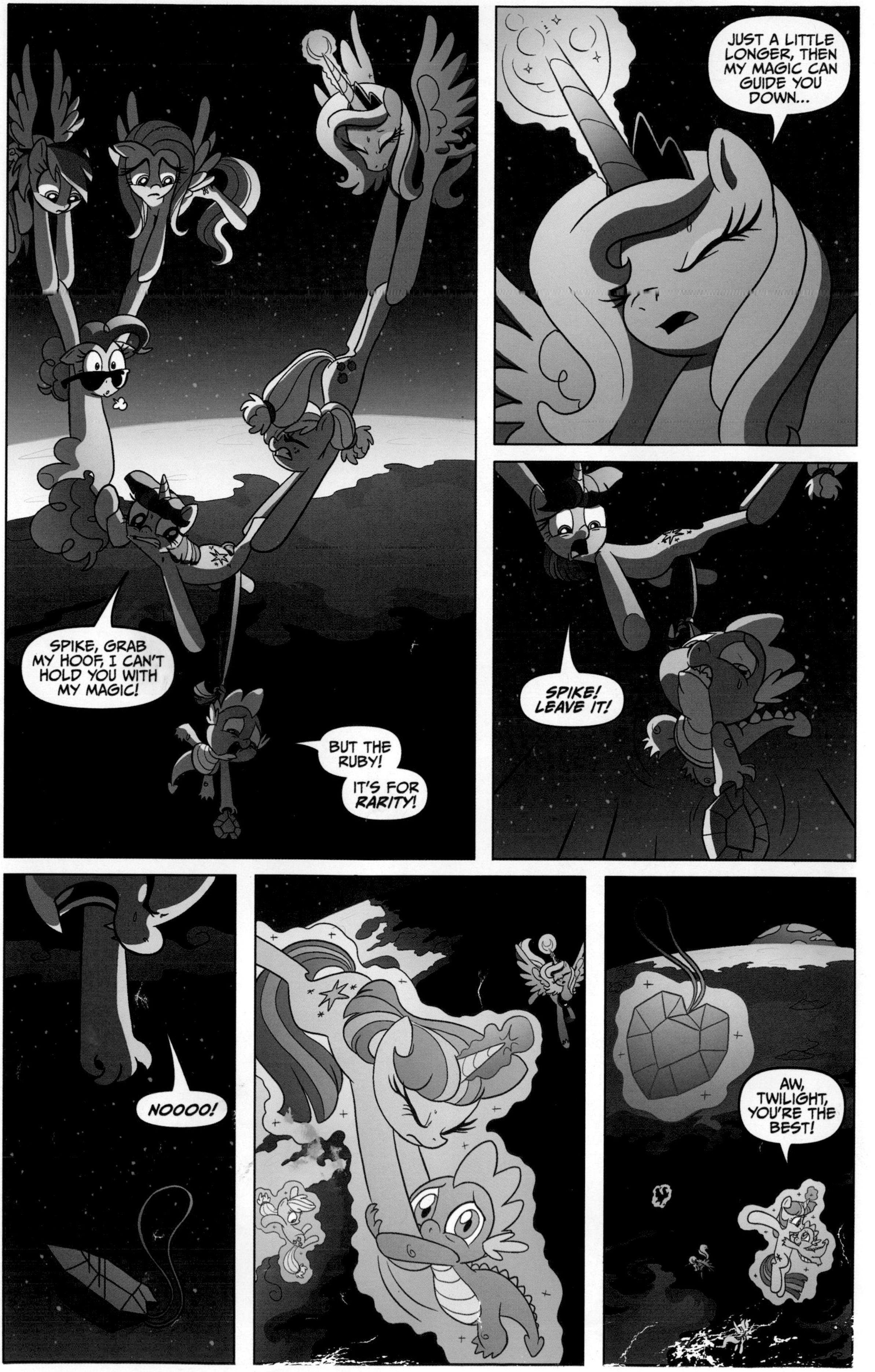

JUST A LITTLE LONGER, THEN MY MAGIC CAN GUIDE YOU DOWN...
SPIKE, GRAB MY HOOF, I CAN'T HOLD YOU WITH MY MAGIC!
BUT THE RUBY!
IT'S FOR *RARITY*!
SPIKE! LEAVE IT!
NOOOO!
AW, TWILIGHT, YOU'RE THE BEST!

FINDING RARITY IN THE PITCH BLACK? NO PROBLEM AT ALL!

WE'LL TAKE CARE OF THAT!

NOW WE MUST HURRY, *THEY'LL* KNOW WE'RE HERE!

AND WHO IS "THEY," EXACTLY?

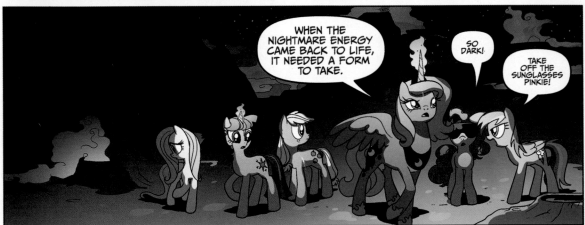

WHEN THE NIGHTMARE ENERGY CAME BACK TO LIFE, IT NEEDED A FORM TO TAKE.

SO DARK!

TAKE OFF THE SUNGLASSES PINKIE!

UNFORTUNATELY, THE PEACEFUL INHABITANTS OF THE MOON BECAME ITS VICTIMS AND ARE NOW TRAPPED UNDER ITS SPELL.

GASP! HOW COULD THEY DO THAT TO SWEET LITTLE ANIMALS?

THEY AREN'T SWEET ANYMORE...

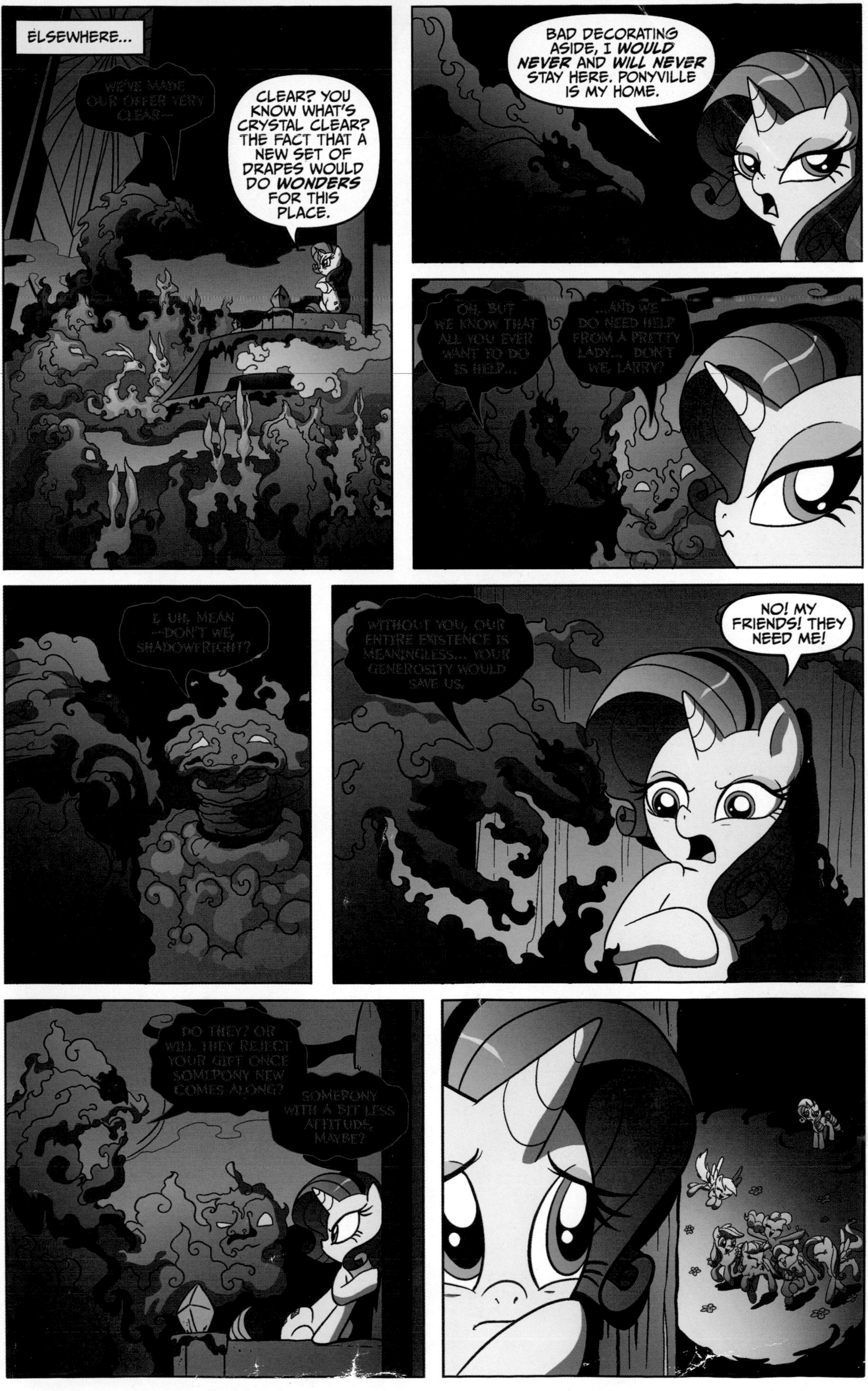
ELSEWHERE...
WE'VE MADE OUR OFFER VERY CLEAR—
CLEAR? YOU KNOW WHAT'S CRYSTAL CLEAR? THE FACT THAT A NEW SET OF DRAPES WOULD DO *WONDERS* FOR THIS PLACE.
BAD DECORATING ASIDE, I *WOULD NEVER* AND *WILL NEVER* STAY HERE. PONYVILLE IS MY HOME.
OH, BUT WE KNOW THAT ALL YOU EVER WANT TO DO IS HELP...
...AND WE DO NEED HELP FROM A PRETTY LADY... DON'T WE, LARRY?
I, UH, MEAN —DON'T WE, SHADOWFRIGHT?
WITHOUT YOU, OUR ENTIRE EXISTENCE IS MEANINGLESS... YOUR GENEROSITY WOULD SAVE US.
NO! MY FRIENDS! THEY NEED ME!
DO THEY? OR WILL THEY REJECT YOUR GIFT ONCE SOMEPONY NEW COMES ALONG?
SOMEPONY WITH A BIT LESS ATTITUDE, MAYBE?

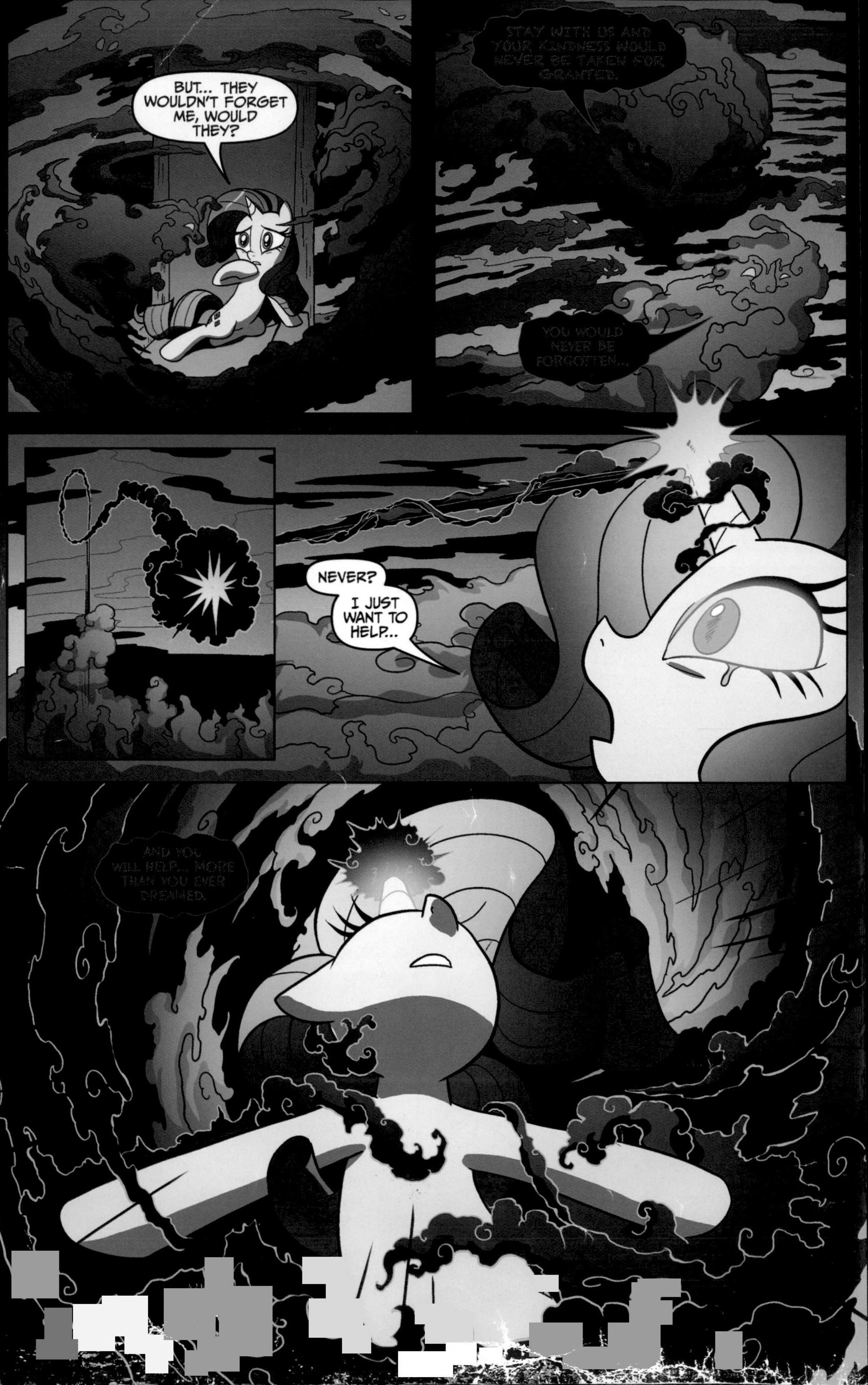
BUT... THEY WOULDN'T FORGET ME, WOULD THEY?
STAY WITH US AND YOUR KINDNESS WOULD NEVER BE TAKEN FOR GRANTED.
YOU WOULD NEVER BE FORGOTTEN...
NEVER? I JUST WANT TO HELP...
AND YOU WILL HELP... MORE THAN YOU EVER DREAMED.

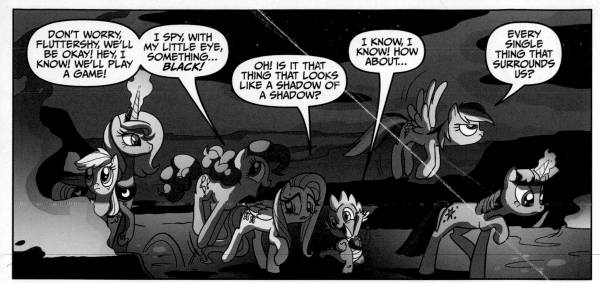

DON'T WORRY, FLUTTERSHY, WE'LL BE OKAY! HEY, I KNOW! WE'LL PLAY A GAME!

I SPY, WITH MY LITTLE EYE, SOMETHING... BLACK!

OH! IS IT THAT THING THAT LOOKS LIKE A SHADOW OF A SHADOW?

I KNOW, I KNOW! HOW ABOUT...

EVERY SINGLE THING THAT SURROUNDS US?

...THAT EXTRA DARK PATCH OF SOMETHING RIGHT BELOW THAT GRAYISH BLOBBY THING?

DING-DING-DING! YOU ARE CORRECT, SIR!

I WAS SO CLOSE.

NOT TO TOOT MY OWN HORN, BUT I AM PRETTY DARN GOOD AT "I SPY."

SPEAKING OF HORNS TOOTING, I THINK THEY DO KNOW WE'RE HERE.

HOW CAN YA TELL?

CALL IT A HUNCH.

WELL, HOWDY THERE, LITTLE CRITTERS WITH YER SPARKLY EYES! WHUDDAYA CALL THAT, FLUTTERSHY?

POSSIBLE INHERENT EVIL?

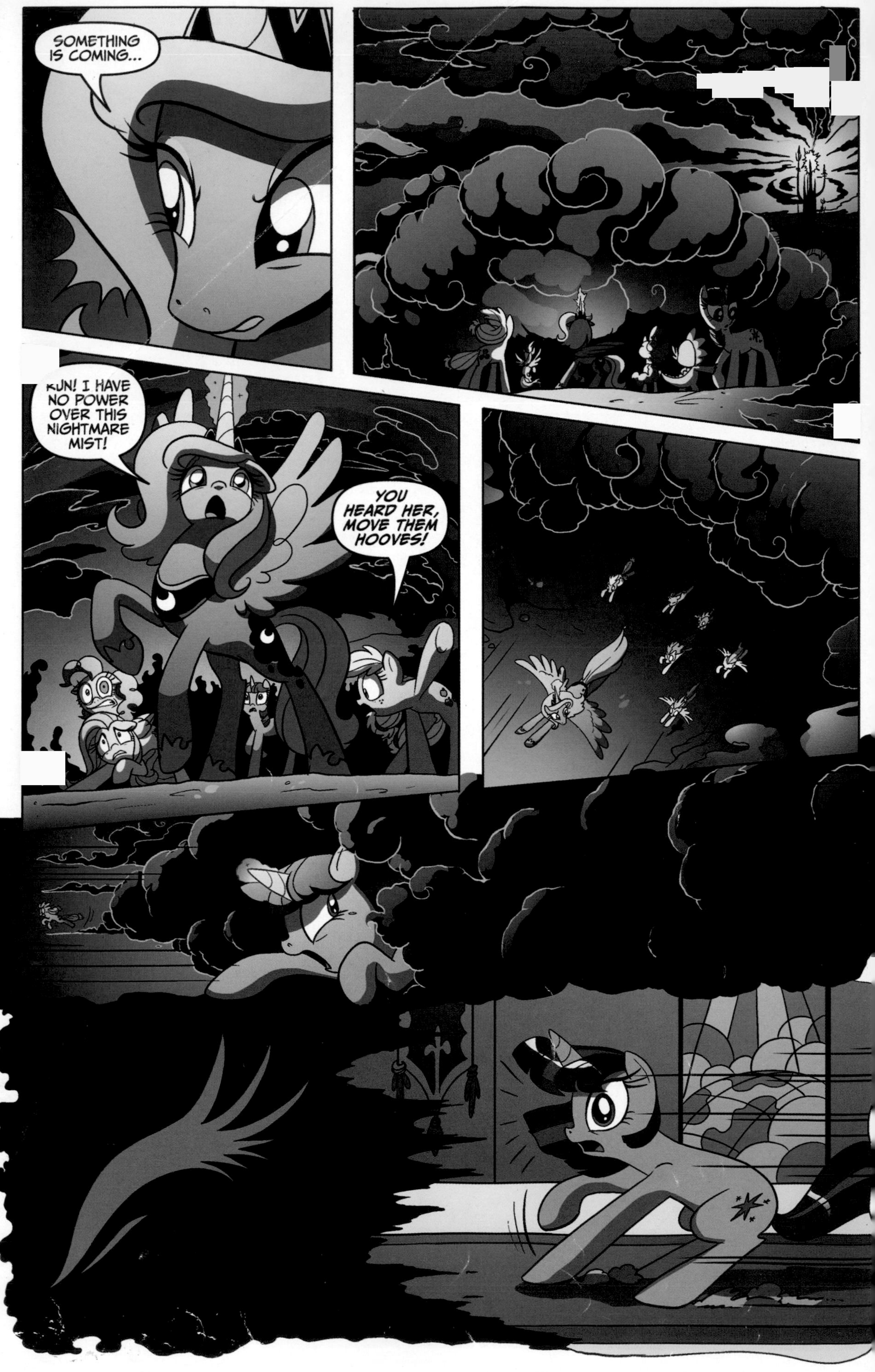
SOMETHING IS COMING...
RUN! I HAVE NO POWER OVER THIS NIGHTMARE MIST!
YOU HEARD HER, MOVE THEM HOOVES!

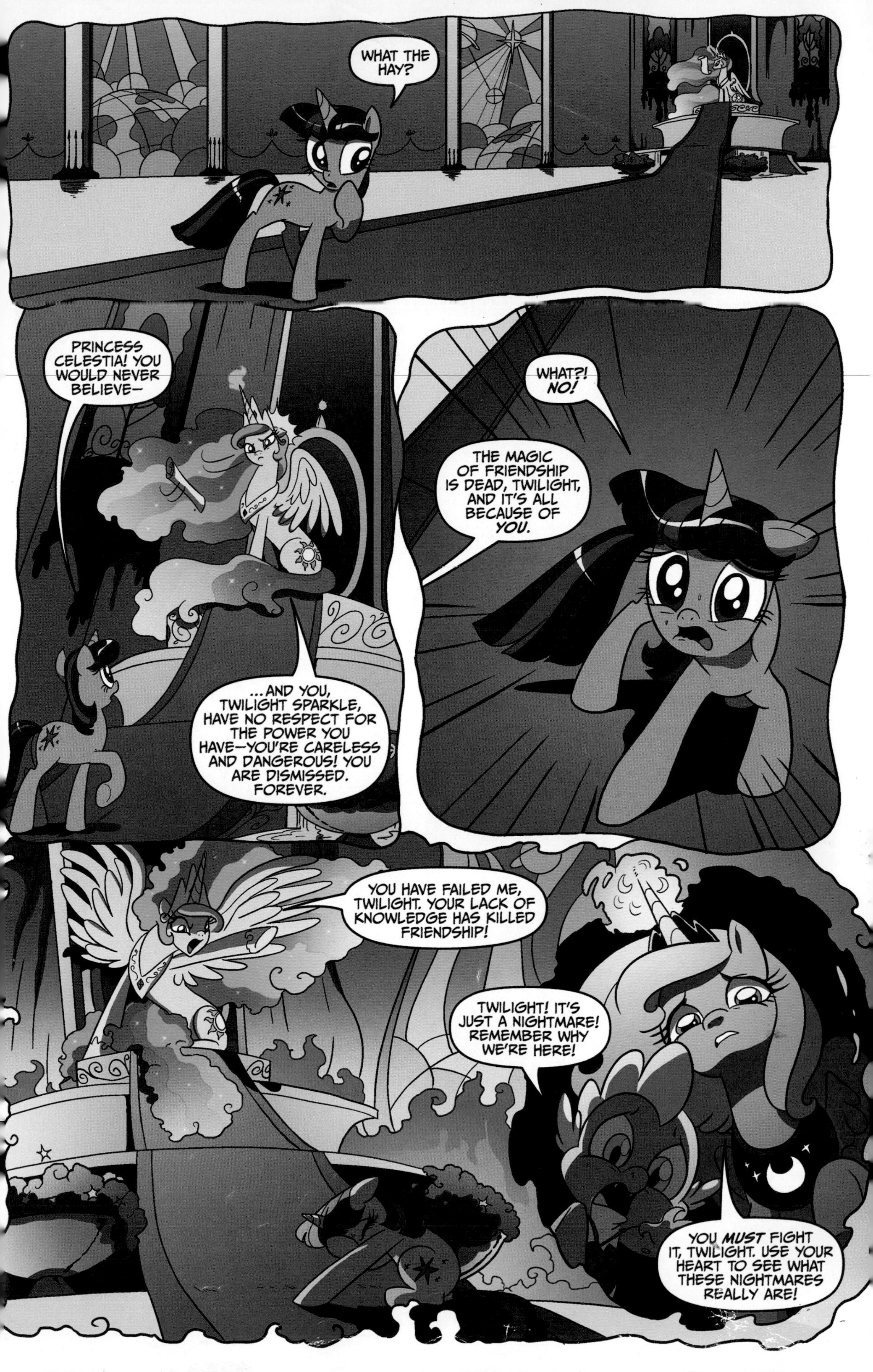
WHAT THE HAY?
PRINCESS CELESTIA! YOU WOULD NEVER BELIEVE—
...AND YOU, TWILIGHT SPARKLE, HAVE NO RESPECT FOR THE POWER YOU HAVE—YOU'RE CARELESS AND DANGEROUS! YOU ARE DISMISSED. FOREVER.
WHAT?! NO!
THE MAGIC OF FRIENDSHIP IS DEAD, TWILIGHT, AND IT'S ALL BECAUSE OF YOU.
YOU HAVE FAILED ME, TWILIGHT. YOUR LACK OF KNOWLEDGE HAS KILLED FRIENDSHIP!
TWILIGHT! IT'S JUST A NIGHTMARE! REMEMBER WHY WE'RE HERE!
YOU MUST FIGHT IT, TWILIGHT. USE YOUR HEART TO SEE WHAT THESE NIGHTMARES REALLY ARE!

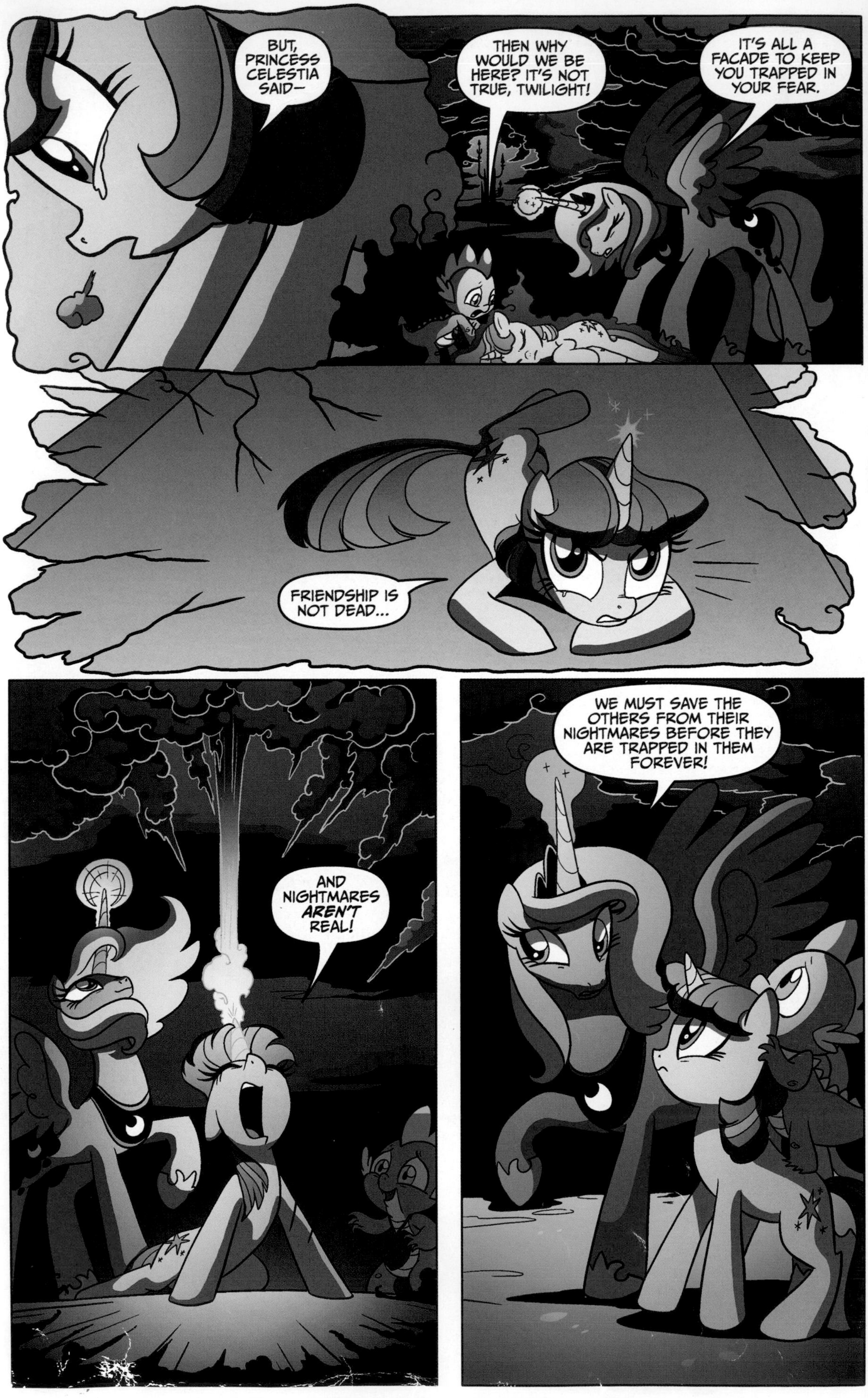
BUT, PRINCESS CELESTIA SAID—
THEN WHY WOULD WE BE HERE? IT'S NOT TRUE, TWILIGHT!
IT'S ALL A FACADE TO KEEP YOU TRAPPED IN YOUR FEAR.
FRIENDSHIP IS NOT DEAD...
AND NIGHTMARES *AREN'T* REAL!
WE MUST SAVE THE OTHERS FROM THEIR NIGHTMARES BEFORE THEY ARE TRAPPED IN THEM FOREVER!

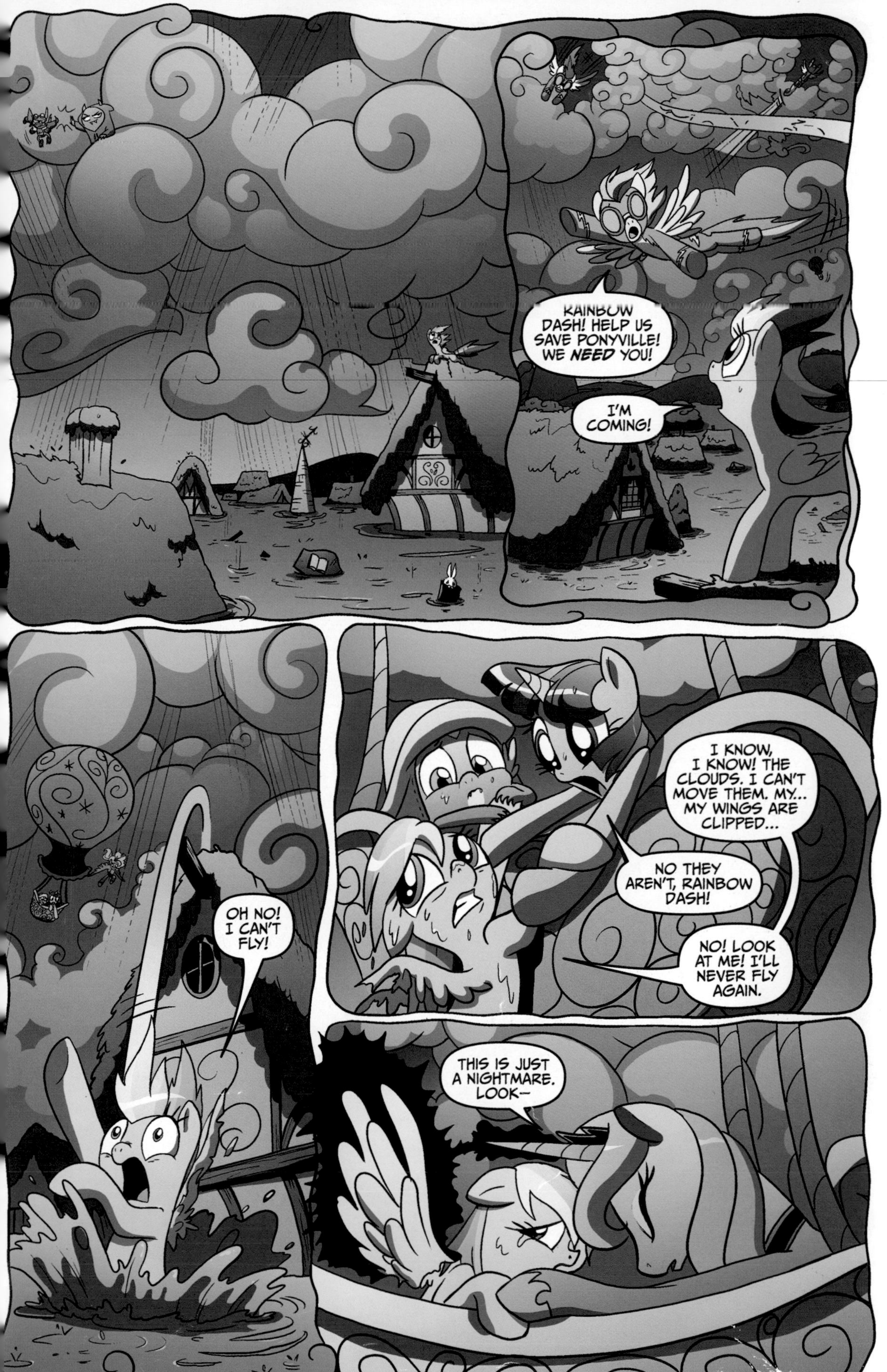
RAINBOW DASH! HELP US SAVE PONYVILLE! WE NEED YOU!
I'M COMING!
OH NO! I CAN'T FLY!
I KNOW, I KNOW! THE CLOUDS. I CAN'T MOVE THEM. MY... MY WINGS ARE CLIPPED...
NO THEY AREN'T, RAINBOW DASH!
NO! LOOK AT ME! I'LL NEVER FLY AGAIN.
THIS IS JUST A NIGHTMARE. LOOK–

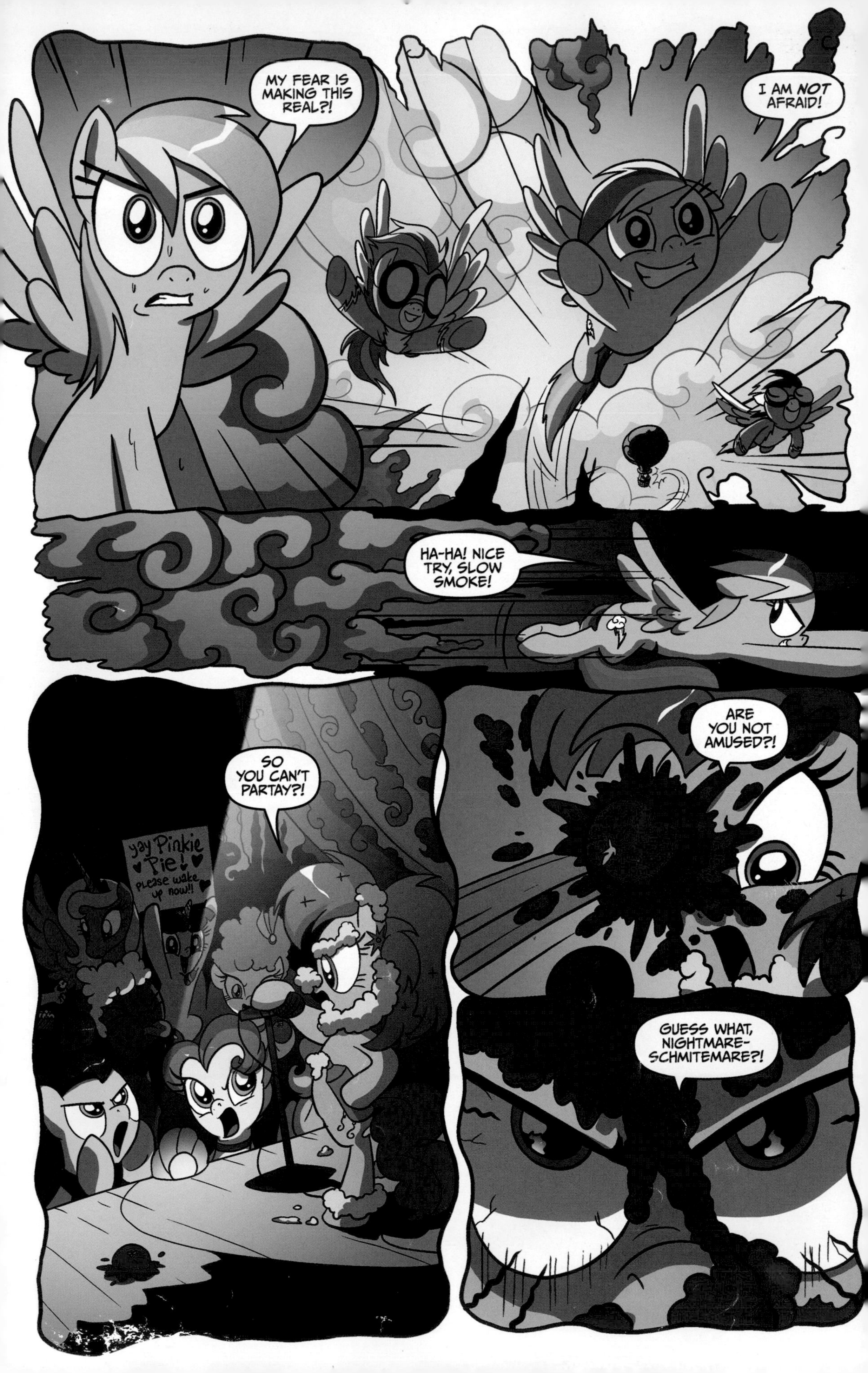
MY FEAR IS MAKING THIS REAL?!
I AM NOT AFRAID!
HA-HA! NICE TRY, SLOW SMOKE!
SO YOU CAN'T PARTAY?!
yay Pinkie Pie! please wake up now!!
ARE YOU NOT AMUSED?!
GUESS WHAT, NIGHTMARE-SCHMITEMARE?!

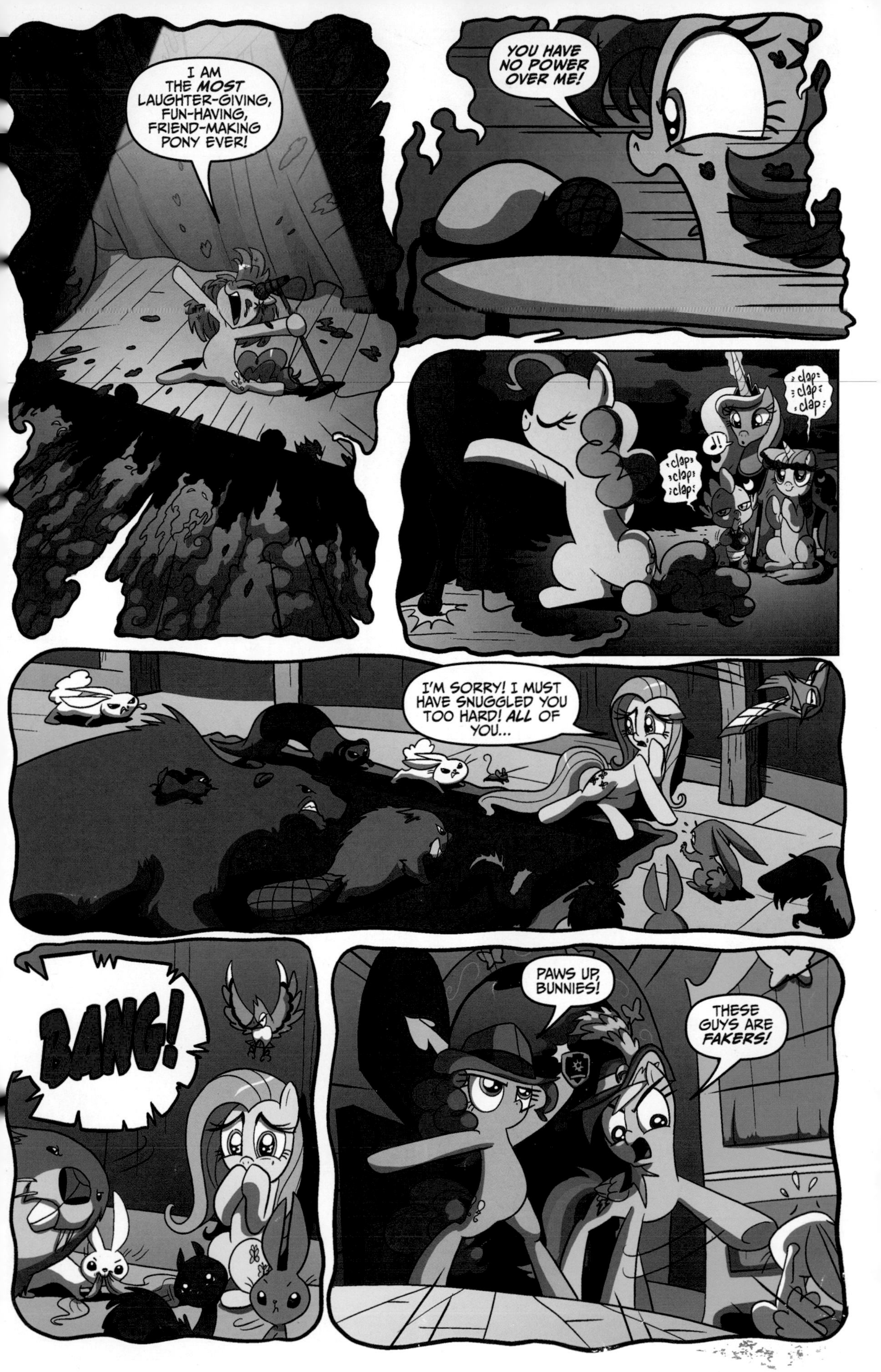

I AM THE *MOST* LAUGHTER-GIVING, FUN-HAVING, FRIEND-MAKING PONY EVER!
YOU HAVE NO POWER OVER ME!
clap clap clap
clap clap clap
I'M SORRY! I MUST HAVE SNUGGLED YOU TOO HARD! *ALL* OF YOU...
BANG!
PAWS UP, BUNNIES!
THESE GUYS ARE *FAKERS!*

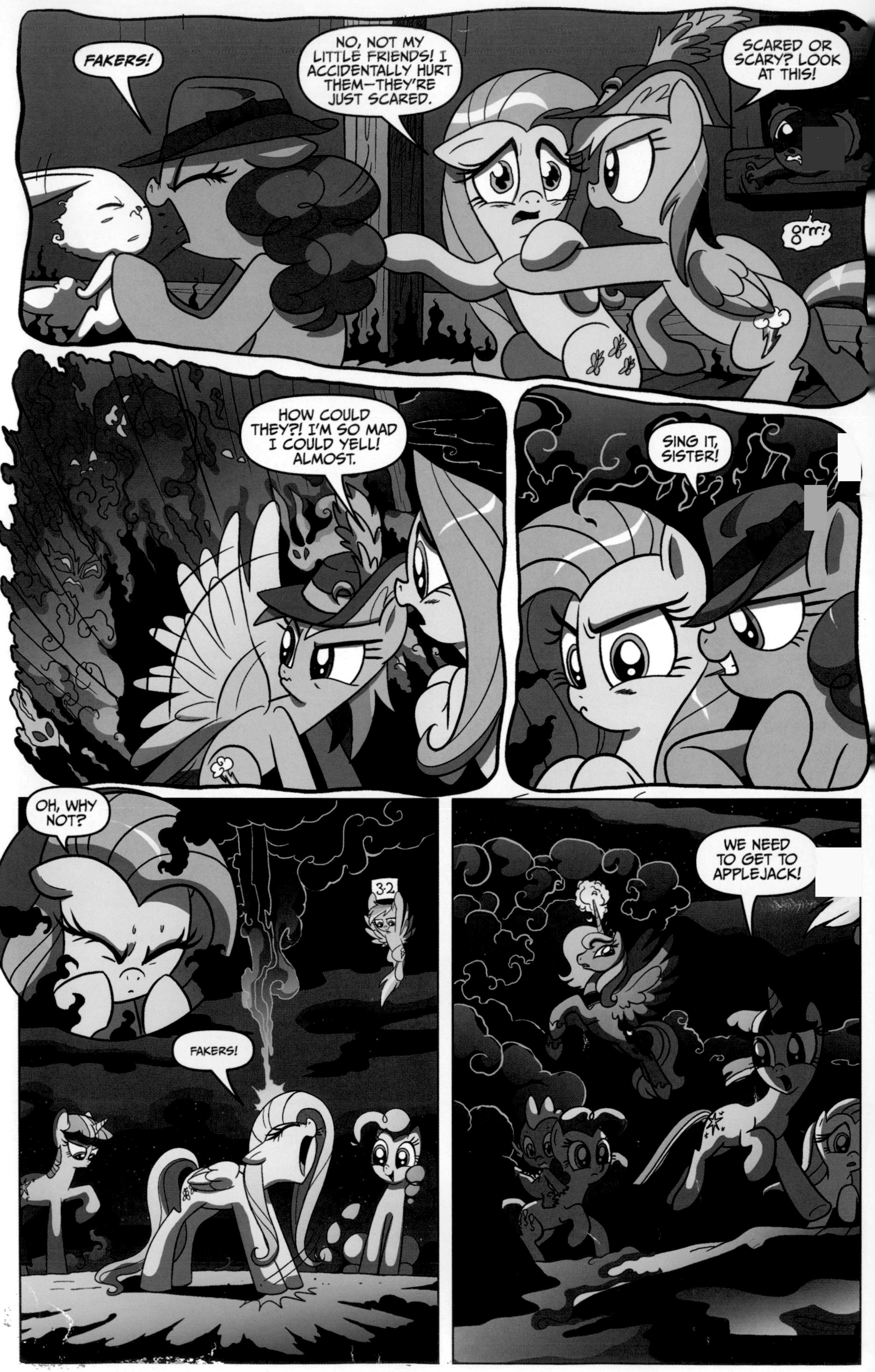
FAKERS!
NO, NOT MY LITTLE FRIENDS! I ACCIDENTALLY HURT THEM—THEY'RE JUST SCARED.
SCARED OR SCARY? LOOK AT THIS!
grrr!
HOW COULD THEY?! I'M SO MAD I COULD YELL! ALMOST.
SING IT, SISTER!
OH, WHY NOT?
FAKERS!
WE NEED TO GET TO APPLEJACK!

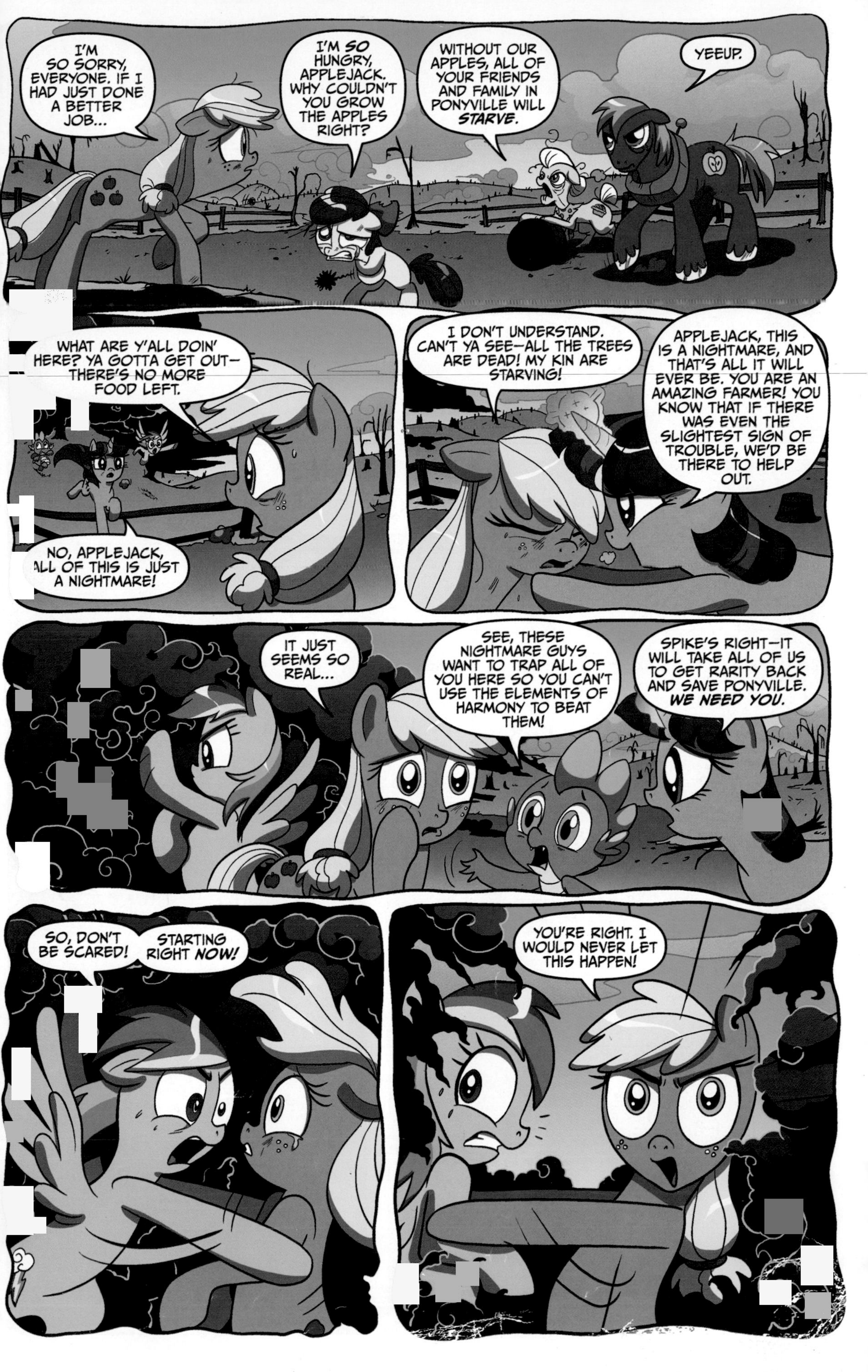
I'M SO SORRY, EVERYONE. IF I HAD JUST DONE A BETTER JOB...
I'M SO HUNGRY, APPLEJACK. WHY COULDN'T YOU GROW THE APPLES RIGHT?
WITHOUT OUR APPLES, ALL OF YOUR FRIENDS AND FAMILY IN PONYVILLE WILL STARVE.
YEEUP.
WHAT ARE Y'ALL DOIN' HERE? YA GOTTA GET OUT—THERE'S NO MORE FOOD LEFT.
NO, APPLEJACK, ALL OF THIS IS JUST A NIGHTMARE!
I DON'T UNDERSTAND. CAN'T YA SEE—ALL THE TREES ARE DEAD! MY KIN ARE STARVING!
APPLEJACK, THIS IS A NIGHTMARE, AND THAT'S ALL IT WILL EVER BE. YOU ARE AN AMAZING FARMER! YOU KNOW THAT IF THERE WAS EVEN THE SLIGHTEST SIGN OF TROUBLE, WE'D BE THERE TO HELP OUT.
IT JUST SEEMS SO REAL...
SEE, THESE NIGHTMARE GUYS WANT TO TRAP ALL OF YOU HERE SO YOU CAN'T USE THE ELEMENTS OF HARMONY TO BEAT THEM!
SPIKE'S RIGHT—IT WILL TAKE ALL OF US TO GET RARITY BACK AND SAVE PONYVILLE. WE NEED YOU.
SO, DON'T BE SCARED!
STARTING RIGHT NOW!
YOU'RE RIGHT. I WOULD NEVER LET THIS HAPPEN!

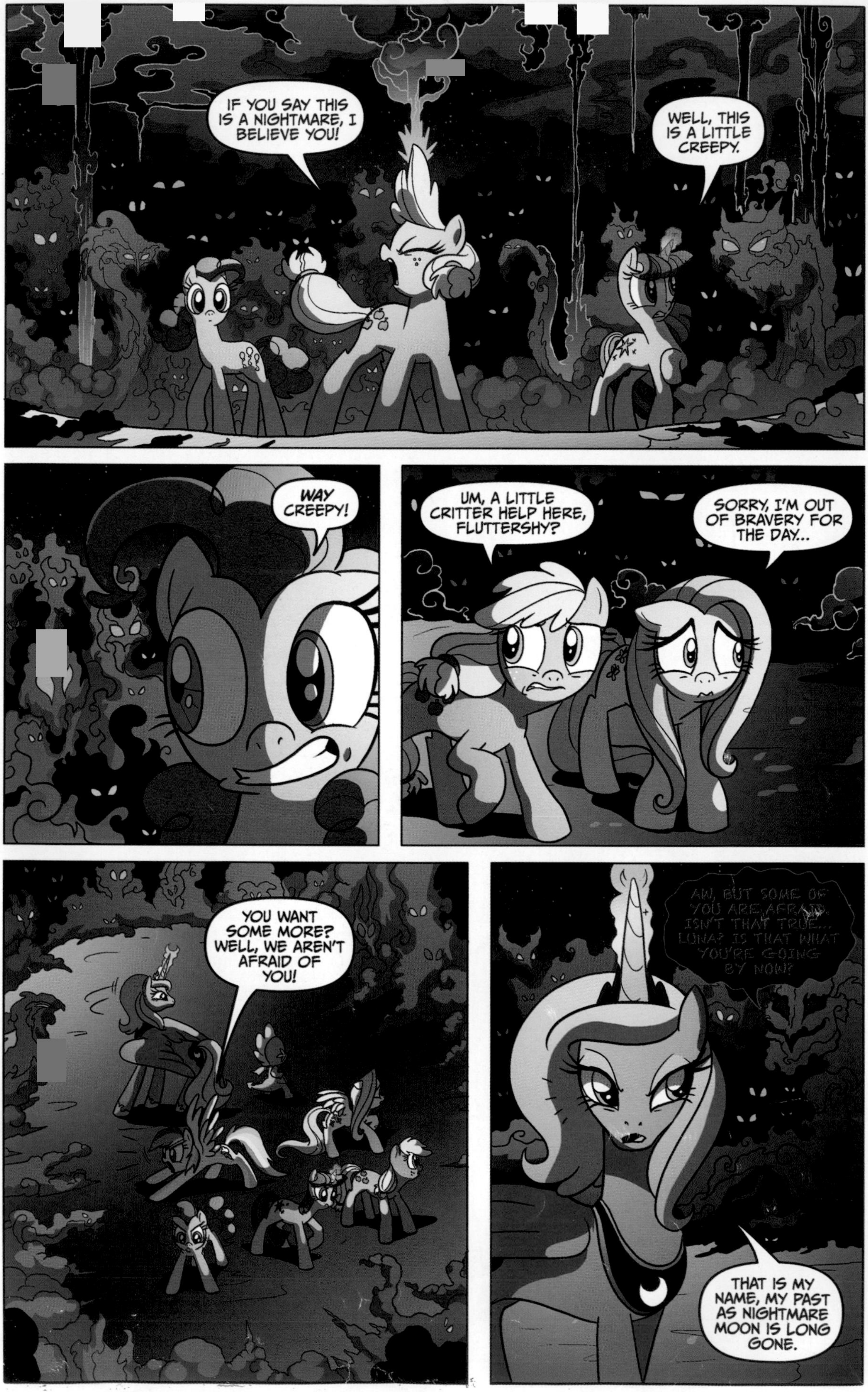
IF YOU SAY THIS IS A NIGHTMARE, I BELIEVE YOU!
WELL, THIS IS A LITTLE CREEPY.
WAY CREEPY!
UM, A LITTLE CRITTER HELP HERE, FLUTTERSHY?
SORRY, I'M OUT OF BRAVERY FOR THE DAY...
YOU WANT SOME MORE? WELL, WE AREN'T AFRAID OF YOU!
AW, BUT SOME OF YOU ARE AFRAID. ISN'T THAT TRUE... LUNA? IS THAT WHAT YOU'RE GOING BY NOW?
THAT IS MY NAME, MY PAST AS NIGHTMARE MOON IS LONG GONE.

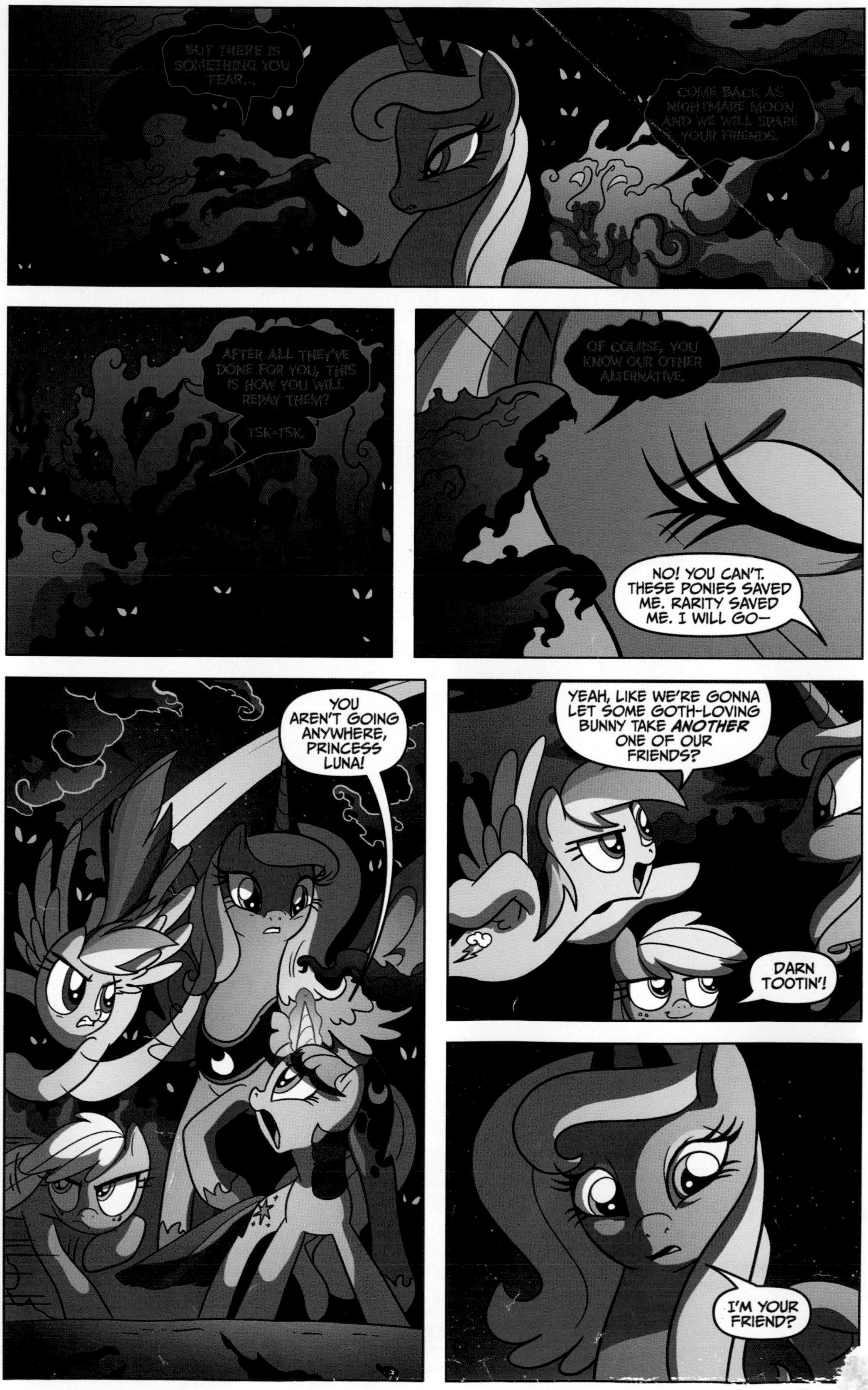
BUT THERE IS SOMETHING YOU FEAR...
COME BACK AS NIGHTMARE MOON AND WE WILL SPARE YOUR FRIENDS.
AFTER ALL THEY'VE DONE FOR YOU, THIS IS HOW YOU WILL REPAY THEM?
TSK-TSK.
OF COURSE, YOU KNOW OUR OTHER ALTERNATIVE.
NO! YOU CAN'T. THESE PONIES SAVED ME. RARITY SAVED ME. I WILL GO—
YOU AREN'T GOING ANYWHERE, PRINCESS LUNA!
YEAH, LIKE WE'RE GONNA LET SOME GOTH-LOVING BUNNY TAKE ANOTHER ONE OF OUR FRIENDS?
DARN TOOTIN'!
I'M YOUR FRIEND?

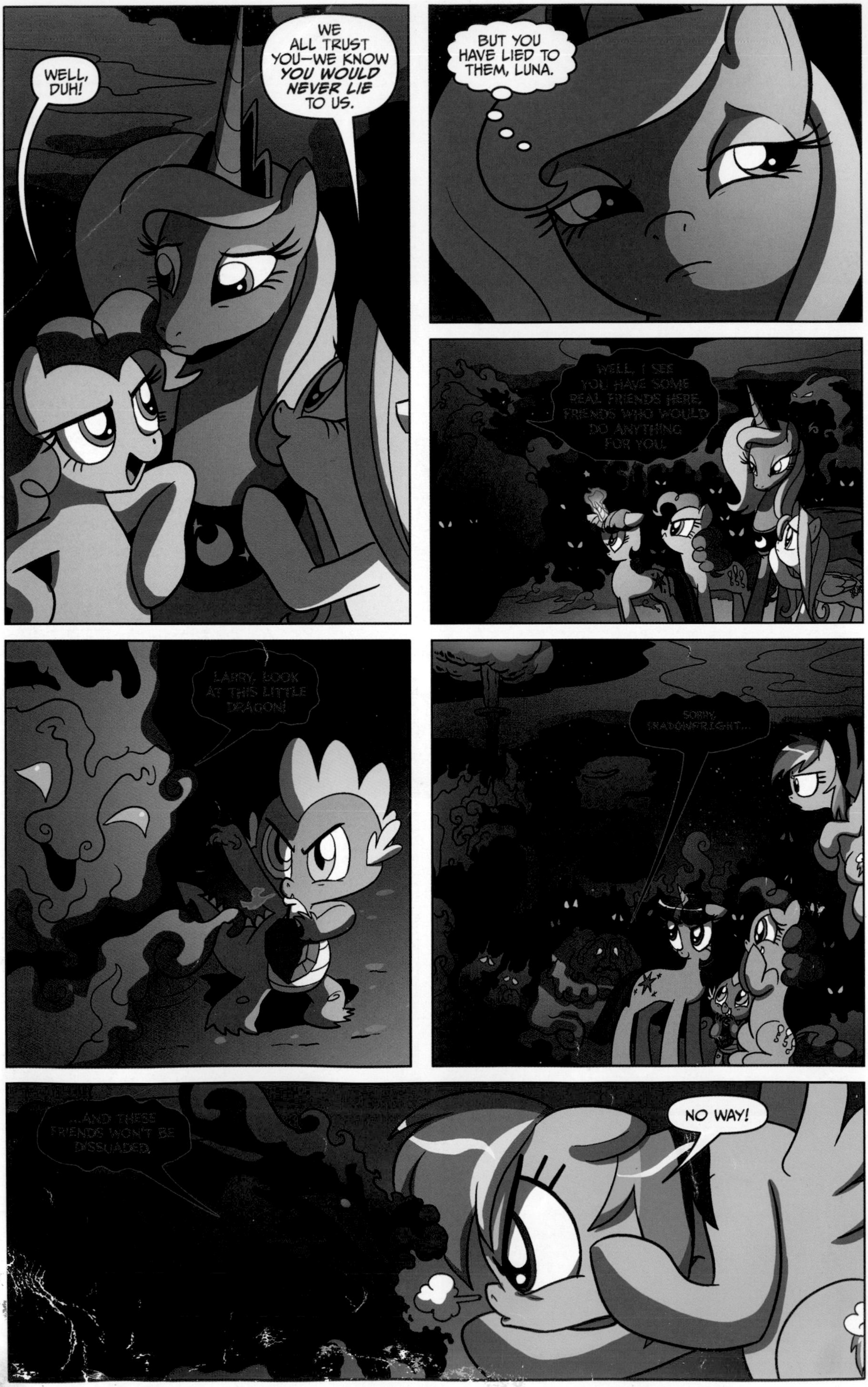
WELL, DUH!
WE ALL TRUST YOU—WE KNOW *YOU WOULD NEVER LIE* TO US.
BUT YOU HAVE LIED TO THEM, LUNA.
WELL, I SEE YOU HAVE SOME REAL FRIENDS HERE, FRIENDS WHO WOULD DO ANYTHING FOR YOU.
LARRY, LOOK AT THIS LITTLE DRAGON!
SORRY, SHADOWFRIGHT...
...AND THESE FRIENDS WON'T BE DISSUADED.
NO WAY!

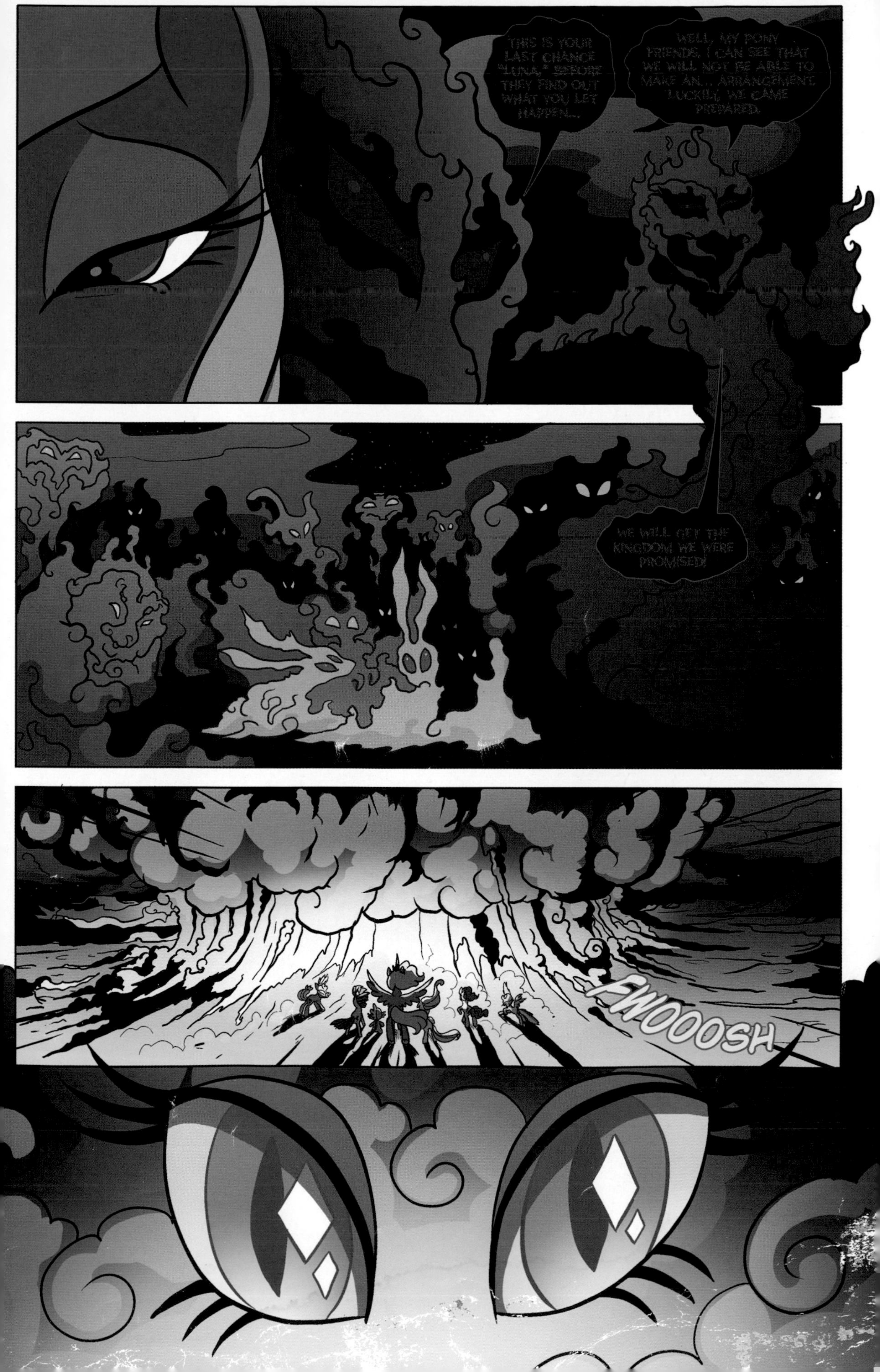
THIS IS YOUR LAST CHANCE "LUNA," BEFORE THEY FIND OUT WHAT YOU LET HAPPEN...
WELL, MY PONY FRIENDS, I CAN SEE THAT WE WILL NOT BE ABLE TO MAKE AN... ARRANGEMENT. LUCKILY, WE CAME PREPARED.
WE WILL GET THE KINGDOM WE WERE PROMISED!
FWOOOSH

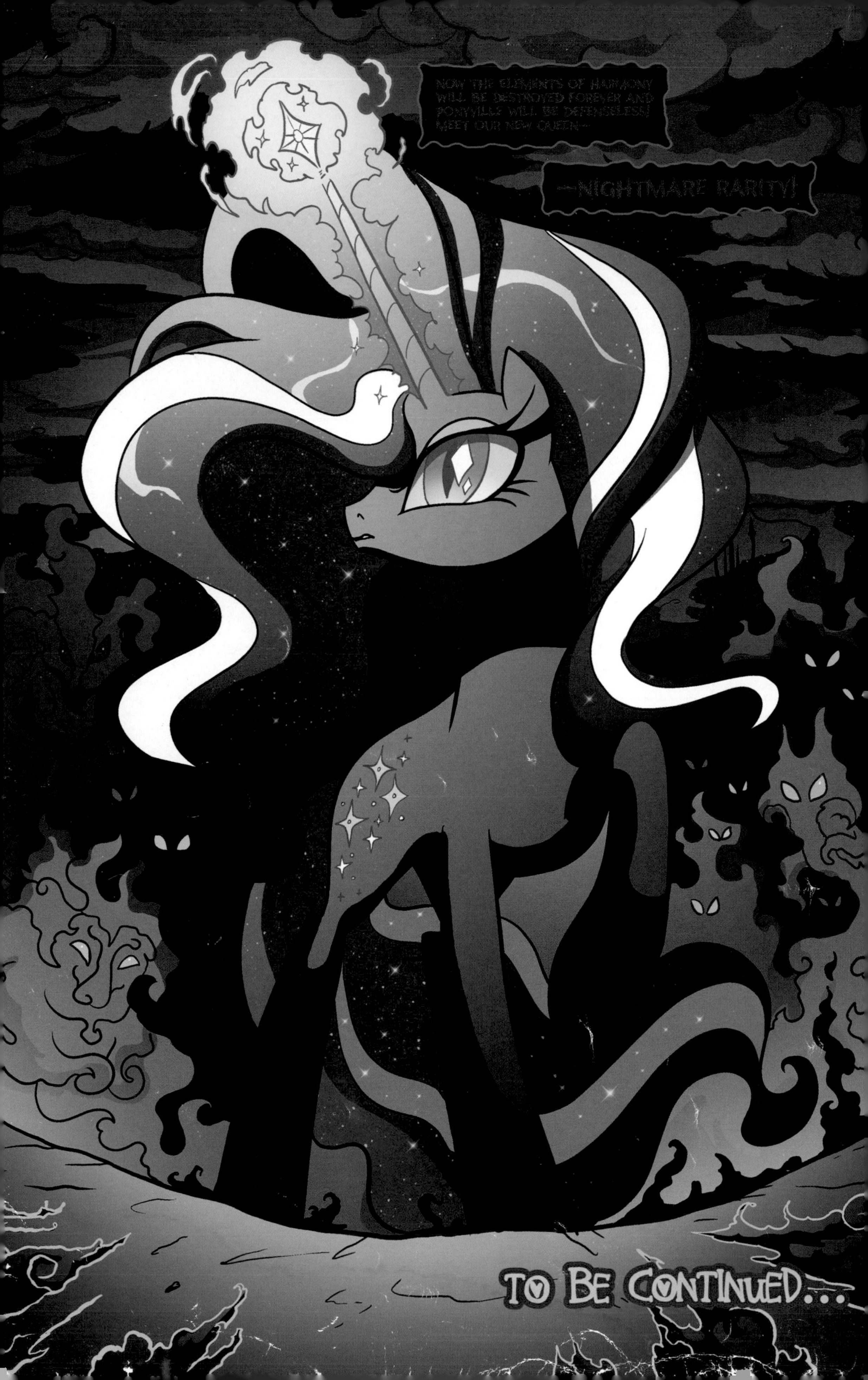
NOW THE ELEMENTS OF HARMONY WILL BE DESTROYED FOREVER AND PONYVILLE WILL BE DEFENSELESS! MEET OUR NEW QUEEN--
--NIGHTMARE RARITY!
TO BE CONTINUED...